# THE WEEBIE ZONE #1

··········································

# Gerbilitis

## by Stephanie Spinner
## and Ellen Weiss

*illustrated by Steve Björkman*

HarperTrophy
*A Division of HarperCollinsPublishers*

*For Wendy and Tom,*
*animal lovers*
—S.S.

*For David*
—S.B.

GERBILITIS
Text copyright © 1996 by Stephanie Spinner and Ellen Weiss
Illustrations copyright © 1996 by Steve Björkman
All rights reserved. No part of this book may be used or
reproduced in any manner whatsoever without written permission except
in the case of brief quotations embodied in critical articles and reviews.
Printed in the United States of America. For information address
HarperCollins Children's Books, a division of HarperCollins Publishers,
10 East 53rd Street, New York, NY 10022.

Library of Congress Cataloging-in-Publication Data
Spinner, Stephanie.
  Gerbilitis / by Stephanie Spinner and Ellen Weiss ; illustrated by Steve Björkman.
      p.      cm. — (The Weebie zone)
  Summary: When Garth takes the class gerbil home for the summer, he discovers
that he can talk not only with Weebie but also with other animals.
  ISBN 0-06-027336-4 (lib. bdg.) — ISBN 0-06-442031-0 (pbk.)
  [1. Gerbils—Fiction.   2. Family life—Fiction.   3. Schools—Fiction]
I. Weiss, Ellen, date.   II. Björkman, Steve, ill.   III. Title.   IV. Series: Spinner,
Stephanie.   Weebie zone.
PZ7.S7567Ge   1996                                                         95-52359
[Fic]—dc20                                                                      CIP
                                                                                AC

1   2   3   4   5   6   7   8   9   10
❖
First Edition

# Contents

# CHAPTER ONE

# Gerbil on the Loose

Weebie was loose again. The class was in an uproar.

"I'll get him!" cried Jeremy, diving under Ms. Wackerow's desk.

"No! He's over here!" called Sarah from the reading corner. "Under the rug!" Everyone rushed over to the reading corner.

Sure enough, a tiny gerbil-sized bump was zigzagging its way from one end of the rug to the other.

"Oh, why do you children keep taking Weebie out of his cage?" wailed Ms. Wackerow.

"This is the third time this week he's run away. One of these days he'll run away for good!"

"Yeah, like that little snake Lester brought in last fall," said Ted. He snickered. "He's probably nine feet long now, down in the basement, eating water bugs."

"Eeeew," screeched Melody.

"Catch him!" yelled Jeremy, pointing at the rug. "He's heading for the door!"

Ted, Garth, and Sarah jumped at the same time, landing in a pile on the floor. Garth stood up first. "Got him," he said with satisfaction, gripping Weebie in his fist.

"Way to go, Garth!" said Jeremy. He opened Weebie's cage.

Garth dropped the gerbil inside. "All righty, Weeb," he said. "Get on your little wheel now." But Weebie just stood there, his tiny paws on the bars of his cage, like a prisoner in a cell. The sight took the smile right off Garth's face. Poor little guy, he thought.

Then Ms. Wackerow tapped on her desk. "Class!" she said, in her pay-attention-or-else

voice. "No more passing that gerbil around—please! From now on one person at a time will come to me for permission. Then that person, and *only* that person, may hold Weebie." She paused for a moment. "Is that clear?"

"Yes, Ms. Wackerow," said the class in a chorus.

"Good." Her voice softened. "Try to remember that Weebie is not a toy, or a beanbag. He is a living creature. And we must treat him with respect."

Loretta raised her hand. "We do respect him, Ms. Wackerow," she said. "But he's so little and warm and soft. And his feet feel so tickly on your hand."

Melody giggled. So did Sarah. Garth crossed his eyes in disgust. Girls!

"I know he feels nice," said Ms. Wackerow, who sometimes picked Weebie up herself. "But we've got to take care of him properly. So—one person at a time. Okay?"

"O-kaaay," answered the class. They all liked Ms. Wackerow, even though she was a little strict. At least she let them have a gerbil. None of the other teachers allowed pets.

So everyone settled down, and for the rest of the afternoon Weebie was forgotten.

When the bell rang at three thirty, Ms. Wackerow reminded everyone about the geography test the next day. There were groans and sighs.

"Don't complain," she said. "It's the last one of the year." Then, as the class streamed out the door, she called Garth's name.

Uh-oh. Was she going to bug him about his spelling again?

"Garth," she said, "I have a big favor to ask you."

He swallowed. Maybe the favor had something to do with studying harder. He hoped not.

"It's about Weebie," she said. "Jeremy was going to take him for the summer, but he can't now—he'll be visiting family out west. So I've got to find someone else. I've asked several other children, but everyone seems to be going away. What about you? Will you be here for the summer?"

Garth nodded.

"Could you take Weebie?"

Garth felt stuck. He liked Weebie all right, but he didn't want to take care of him. Besides, Weebie's cage smelled like the monkey house at the zoo.

Ms. Wackerow smiled at Garth hopefully. He sighed. It was true, he was going to be in Duanesville all summer. He knew that for sure, because his mother was working full-time at her psychologist job *and* going to graduate school. When she was done, she'd be called *Doctor* Hunter. If she ever got done, which Garth doubted.

Meanwhile, they were stuck at home for the summer. Again. And Garth was going to day camp, which he hated like poison.

"I'll have to ask my parents," he told his teacher.

"That would be lovely," she said.

That night Garth tried to find a good moment to ask his parents about Weebie, but it was hard. There didn't seem to be any good moments. Not these days, realized Garth. They were always crabbing about something, usually while they ate. Like now.

"I thought you said you'd be home early tonight," said Garth's father.

"Did I?" said Garth's mother. "Oh. Well. One of my patients had a crisis, so we were on the phone for an hour. That threw my whole schedule off, so everyone else ran late. Then I couldn't find the notes for my paper ..." She sighed, looking guilty. "You know how it is."

Garth's father spooned macaroni and cheese onto three plates. "Sure I know. I just can't get used to it, that's all." He passed the plates, then took a bite of his food and winced. "Mmm. Another delicious home-microwaved meal."

"Toby," said Garth's mother. "Please." That meant, Please don't give me a hard time in front of Garth. Wait until later, when he's upstairs in bed, trying not to listen to us argue.

Garth chewed his macaroni and cheese, which tasted like the stuff in the school cafeteria. Maybe a little worse. His parents said nothing for a while.

In the silence Joan, the cat, jumped onto the kitchen counter and sniffed the macaroni container. Then she started to lick it.

"Joan! Get down from there!" yelled Garth's father.

Garth's mother stopped eating. "Don't yell at her, please," she said.

"Don't yell at her! What should I do, send her a fax?" snorted Garth's father.

"Maybe she wouldn't be on the counter if she got fed every now and then," Garth's mother snapped. "She's probably hungry."

Joan meowed loudly, as if she were agreeing. Feeding her wasn't exactly anybody's job, so she just got fed when somebody noticed that her bowl was empty. Now she glared at them with her huge, blue, crossed eyes, and meowed again. Getting no response, she jumped off the counter and stalked out of the kitchen.

"I'll feed you later, Joanie," Garth's mother called after the cat. "I promise." Then she turned to Garth.

"So how was your day at school, sweetheart?"

"Fine."

"Just fine? Did anything actually *happen*?"

"Well, one thing happened," said Garth, realizing this was his chance. "Ms. Wackerow asked me if I would take Weebie home for the summer."

"Weebie?" said Garth's father. "Who's Weebie?"

"Our gerbil," said Garth.

"What exactly is a gerbil?" Garth's mother asked him. "Is it one of those furry things that looks like a bedroom slipper?"

"No, Mom, that's a guinea pig," said Garth. "A gerbil is little. About like a big mouse."

"A big *mouse*?" A look of alarm crossed his mother's face.

"But much cuter," said Garth quickly.

"Well . . . we could think about it," said his mother. "If it will help your teacher out."

"Do you want to have Dweebie for the summer?" asked his father.

"Weebie, Dad," corrected Garth. The image of the gerbil gripping the bars of his cage popped into Garth's mind. He'd looked so sad.

"I guess it would be okay," said Garth.

And that was how Weebie came to Garth's house.

........................................................

# CHAPTER TWO

# Someone New Speaks Up

The first problem was where to put Weebie's cage.

Garth was not a neat boy. In fact, he was probably the messiest boy in the state of Connecticut. There was a blue carpet on his floor, but not a square inch of it showed. It was completely covered with stuff—books, clothes, tapes, pencils, crayons, trading cards, shoes, comics, maps, action figures, and magazines. So was the desk, and so was the bed, though Garth did keep one corner clear for sleeping. Overall, there wasn't much room for a gerbil, let alone a gerbil in a big wire cage.

After standing in the middle of his room holding Weebie's cage for fifteen minutes, Garth decided that drastic action was called for. He swept half the stuff on his desk onto the floor. Then he set Weebie's cage down.

"There you go, little dude," he said. "Home."

Weebie scurried to a corner and looked around nervously.

Just then Joan sauntered in, looking bored. Halfway to the bed she stopped, her muscles rigid. She had smelled Weebie.

Then she was on the desk, crouched in front of his cage with her tail twitching, like a hungry lion getting ready to go after a gazelle. She meowed softly, eyes narrowed. Weebie huddled in his corner and did not move. Garth could tell he was terrified.

"Forget it, Joan," he told the cat. "This is not a meal. This is a pet."

Joan's tail thrashed across the desk like an angry snake. A scary noise came from the back of her throat.

"Scat!" ordered Garth, waving his arms at her. "I mean it!"

Joan took her time about jumping off the desk. As she strolled out of the room, Garth said, "Don't worry, Weebie. I won't let her eat you."

Weebie huddled motionless at the back of his cage. He was so still, he could have passed for a stuffed toy, thought Garth. "Weeb, dude?" he asked. "You okay?"

There was no response. Garth shrugged. He closed his bedroom door firmly to keep Joan out, and went downstairs to watch television until his dad got home.

Mr. Hunter always got home before Mrs. Hunter. He had a design studio in town; her office was in the city. And she always seemed to work longer hours than he did. These days she almost never showed up before seven thirty, and when she did, she was always tired.

Garth's father came home at six. "Mom call yet?" he asked, turning down the television.

"Nope," said Garth.

His father started poking around in the refrigerator for something to make for dinner. "Congratulations on your last day of school," he called from the kitchen.

"Thanks," said Garth.

"You bring that gerbil home with you?" He stood in the doorway, wiping his hands on a towel.

"Yup."

"Well, let's have a look at him." They went up to Garth's room. Weebie was still in his corner. He hadn't moved, as far as Garth could tell.

"He's a cute little guy," said Mr. Hunter. Weebie wiggled his nose in a cute way.

Mr. Hunter leaned down and looked into Weebie's cage. "Where's his water?" he asked Garth.

"Oops," said Garth. "I forgot he needs water."

"And what about his food?" asked Mr. Hunter. "Didn't you give him any lettuce or anything?"

Garth blushed. He'd forgotten that, too.

"You'll have to do a little better than this,"

said Mr. Hunter. "Or you'll be giving Ms. Wackerow a dead gerbil in the fall. Which is probably not what she wants, if I know Ms. Wackerow."

Garth imagined carrying a little wooden coffin back to school in September and handing it to his teacher. He could just see the look of horror on her face.

"Okay, okay," he told his father. "I'll take care of him."

In the next few days Garth tried to do better, but he still made mistakes. He'd remember Weebie's water, but he'd forget his food. Or he'd give him food but forget to change the shredded newspaper at the bottom of his cage. "Sorry, Weeb," he'd say as he ran to catch the bus to day camp, or hurried out to a softball game. "Gotta go, little dude."

One night after about a week of this, when Garth stuck his hand into Weebie's cage to put down a lettuce leaf, Weebie bit him. His teeth were tiny but sharp.

"OW!" yelled Garth. "That hurt!" His hand stung, and suddenly his head felt funny, like it did when his ears popped.

"Good," said Weebie. "I meant it to. My teeth are a lot sharper than your pathetic little brain."

"Yeah, well, you'd better not do that again, because—"

Garth stopped.

*Had Weebie talked to him?*

"Did you talk to me?" he asked the gerbil.

"Yes, I talked to you," snapped Weebie.

Garth sat down on his bed. He was just the slightest bit dizzy.

"How come I can understand you?"

"How should I know?" Weebie's high-pitched, warbly voice was kind of pretty, in spite of the things he was saying.

Garth stared at him, amazed. Now that Garth could understand him, Weebie looked different. Smarter, somehow. His face even had an expression on it. A peeved expression.

Garth closed his mouth and sat there. He

thought of something Ms. Wackerow said every now and then: "Class, gather your wits about you." Garth tried to gather his wits, but they were scattered all over the place. Maybe I'm dreaming, he thought.

"This isn't real," he said. "It can't be."

"You bet your boots it's real," said Weebie.

So he wasn't dreaming.

Garth thought about it some more. He wondered why he could understand Weebie now, but not when he had first brought him home. Then it hit him. "You bit me!" he cried. "Something happened when you bit me!"

"Maybe," said Weebie. "Maybe you're not such a dimwit after all."

"You could be a little nicer," said Garth.

"Nicer?" squeaked Weebie. "Nicer? These are the words of a boy who throws me a shred of lettuce when he feels like it. Who gives me a droplet of water when the mood strikes him. I would be better off living in the Sahara Desert! Nicer? Huh!" Weebie turned his furry little back in disgust.

"Gee," said Garth. "I'm sorry."

But Weebie wasn't finished complaining. "Even in Ms. Wackerow's class I got fed on time," he griped. "Here it's anybody's guess. Look at me! I've lost a tenth of an ounce already! I'm wasting away!"

"I'm really, really sorry," Garth said, and he meant it. "I'll do a lot better. I promise."

Weebie softened up a little. "Well, I hope so," he said.

Garth shook his head. "I can't believe I'm sitting here talking to a gerbil," he said. "I've got to go tell my dad."

"Ah-ah-ah," cautioned Weebie. "Better not."

"Why not? This is so incredible. Shouldn't I tell my parents about it?"

"I don't think so," said Weebie. "After all, I didn't bite *them*. They can't understand me. They might think you were nuts."

"My mother says we should never use that word," said Garth primly. He thought for a moment. "But you might be right. I better not tell them."

"For now," said Weebie. "Anyway, this whole thing might blow over in an hour or two.

Who knows? You could stop understanding me all of a sudden. Then you could just pretend it was a dream."

"Some dream," said Garth.

Weebie scurried up to the bars of his cage. "In the meantime, do you think you could let me out for a while? I'm feeling awfully cooped up."

"Sure," said Garth. Then he stopped. "This isn't some kind of a trick, is it? You're not going to run away, are you?"

Weebie looked at him. "Where would I run to?"

"You were always running away in school."

"That was different. I was trying to get to the science room. I heard there were white mice there. You know—someone I could talk to."

Garth opened Weebie's cage without another word and carried him over to the bed. Weebie darted around, looking things over.

"What a mess!" he said finally. "You really ought to clean this—"

He froze, eyes on the door. "Quick!" he squeaked. "Hide me! She's back!"

Garth turned. Joan the cat was slinking through the doorway, tail waving.

"Scat! Shoo! Get out of here!" yelled Garth, snatching Weebie up off the bed. He threw a wad of dirty socks at Joan, who stopped in her tracks and hissed at Garth—something she'd never done before. Then she ran out of the room.

Garth was shaken. So was Weebie. "Yow! That was close," he squeaked. "She's *really* after me."

"I won't let her get you. I promise."

"Sure, sure."

"No. Really. When you're in your cage, I'll keep the door to my room shut. Otherwise I'll carry you with me. In my pocket or my pack. Okay?"

"Okay. That's good."

Garth gave Weebie's head a pat with his finger. It wasn't too long before the little guy stopped shaking.

# Weebie Settles In

As soon as Garth got home from camp the next day, he popped Weebie into his waist pack and rode his bike downtown. He'd decided that if he was going to treat Weebie better, he should buy him a few things at the pet shop.

Garth had eight dollars saved up from his allowance. He made up his mind to spend it all, and looked at every single thing in the gerbil-and-hamster section. He finally settled on a new water bottle with a rubber drinking tube, a bigger, better running wheel, a bag of fresh-smelling cedar chips, and a box of Joyous Gerbil

gerbil food. Weebie wanted a little mermaid from one of the tropical fish tanks, but Garth put his foot down.

"We have to make some choices here," he said as quietly as he could. "This is cleaning me out."

"All right, all right," said Weebie. "But do me a favor and get Nacho-Cheese Joyous Gerbil, okay? I hate Joyous Gerbil Classic. It tastes like erasers."

"Demanding, aren't you?" whispered Garth. But he felt great paying for everything with his own money.

When they got home, Garth gave Weebie's cage a good cleaning. He threw out the shredded newspaper and covered the cage bottom with cedar chips. He polished the bars of the cage until they gleamed.

While he worked, Weebie chatted. He was in a much better mood now that Garth was really taking care of him.

"I'll bet you don't know half of what goes on in Ms. Wackerow's class," he said.

"Sure I do," said Garth. "What do you think I am, stupid?"

"Let's not get into that," said Weebie. "But seriously, I'll bet there's a lot you don't know. Like who cheats on tests, for example."

"What!" Garth was shocked. "Nobody cheats!"

"Oh yes they do. Pete and Sarah check each other's spelling answers. And sometimes they write things on their hands."

"No!"

"Yes," said Weebie with pleasure. He loved to gossip, that was clear.

Garth kept polishing. After a while he said, "What else do you know?"

Weebie tried his new water bottle. Then he stepped on and off his new wheel a few times. Finally he said, "Lots, actually. I know what the teachers do after school. Bet you can't guess."

Garth tried, but he just couldn't come up with anything. "All right, I give up," he said after a minute.

"They sit around Ms. Wackerow's classroom and talk about the kids."

"They do?" said Garth in amazement and horror.

"They do," Weebie echoed smugly. "Sometimes they even make fun of them. They do imitations. Some of them are pretty funny."

"That's gross!"

"It's no worse than what the kids say about the teachers when the teachers aren't around," said Weebie reasonably.

"But they're grown-ups!" protested Garth.

"Hah!" snorted Weebie. "They act the same as kids."

"What else?" demanded Garth.

"I could tell you what Ms. Wackerow does when she's all alone marking tests."

"Tell!"

"Only if you buy me that mermaid for my cage."

"You set me up for this!" exclaimed Garth. He didn't know whether to be indignant or impressed.

"Take it or leave it." Weebie looked pleased with himself.

"Okay! As soon as I get some more money. What does she do?"

"She sings Beatles songs," said Weebie. "At the top of her lungs."

"Whoa!" This completely changed the way Garth thought of Ms. Wackerow.

"Her favorite is 'Maxwell's Silver Hammer.' I know the words by heart, thanks to her. 'Bang, bang, Maxwell's silver hammer came down on her head, doop de doo, doo—' " warbled Weebie.

Garth whooped and doubled over with laughter. For the next hour he listened to Weebie's stories of what went on at school, hardly able to believe what he was hearing. Weebie knew about the kids. He knew about the teachers and the principal. He knew about Screamin' Joe Bonano, the bad-tempered custodian. He even knew what the school cooks put in the lunchroom's worst dish, Tuna Surprise.

Garth was awestruck. All this time he'd thought Weebie was just a dopey little furball, running around on a wheel. But nothing could have been further from the truth. Weebie was sharp. He didn't miss a thing.

That night at dinner Garth looked out the kitchen window as he ate with his parents. Some birds—sparrows?—were hopping around on a tree branch. A squirrel hurried up the tree trunk to parts unknown. Garth found himself watching them in a whole new way. What were they saying to each other? Did they have opinions about the people inside the house?

"Garth, take some broccoli," said his mother.

"I already had a piece."

"Have another piece."

"I have an announcement," said Garth's father, brandishing a broccoli stalk. "We are taking a weekend off this summer. Since we can't take a real vacation, we're going away for a weekend. Someplace fun."

Mrs. Hunter's face tightened. "I really don't

think I can get away right now," she said. "Even for a weekend. You know how much pressure I'm under."

"Nola, come on," said Mr. Hunter. "*Anybody* can go away for a weekend."

Garth's mother was dishing out mashed potatoes. She shook the spoon a little harder than she had to. A big glob of the stuff landed on her husband's plate. "Let's talk about this later," she said, frowning.

They ate in silence after that. As soon as he'd finished, Garth asked to be excused.

"Before dessert?" asked Mr. Hunter, surprised.

"Not hungry," said Garth.

"Okay, go ahead."

Back in his room he found Weebie on his new wheel, running so fast that the wheel hummed. After a minute it slowed and then stopped. Weebie hopped off and did a few stretches.

"I needed that," he told Garth, breathing hard. "Now, how about some television?"

"You like television?" asked Garth.

"Well, I've never seen it, since I've lived in a classroom for most of my life. But I've heard a lot about it, and I'm curious."

"Sure," said Garth. "Let's go." He popped Weebie into the pocket of his T-shirt, and they went down to the den.

"What would you like to see?" he asked Weebie, picking up the remote control.

"Oh, I don't know. Something with a lot of hitting and killing."

"Plenty to choose from there," said Garth, turning the set on. He began flipping channels. "Here's a good one," he said. A big man was hitting a little man over the head with a golf club.

Weebie, who was peeking over the top of Garth's pocket, squeaked in distress. "Yikes! Why do people like this stuff?"

Garth changed the channel and got a nature program. A lion was stalking a herd of zebras. It crept along toward them, tail flicking.

"Oh, this is much better," said Weebie. "Nice and nonviolent."

At that moment Joan bounded onto the sofa

and sat next to Garth, flicking her tail. Her eyes were glued to his pocket.

Garth realized that she looked exactly like the lion on television. "Don't even think about it," he warned.

"Why not?" she asked silkily.

"Because, because . . ." he sputtered. "Because it's a really mean thing to do, and—*Hey!*"

Her huge blue eyes looked up at him innocently.

"I can talk to you, too!" he exclaimed.

"So it seems," said Joan. Then her eyes went back to his pocket, where Weebie was hunched in a corner, trembling.

"You won't let her get me, will you?" he squeaked.

Joan started purring. "Just let me nibble on his little toes," she coaxed.

"No!" yelped Garth.

"Pretty please?"

"Out of the question!" He picked up a pillow and batted at her with it until she jumped off the

sofa. "I'm already sorry I can understand you," he told her. "Keep away from him!"

Garth's father appeared in the doorway. "Were you talking to somebody?" he asked.

Garth sat down on the sofa, completely flustered. "Uh, no . . . I was just, ah . . . talking to myself," he said.

"Uh-oh," said his father. "That's a sure sign you're going crazy." A guilty look passed over his face. He and Garth both knew that Mrs. Hunter didn't like the word "crazy," either. "I mean, losing your mind. Oh, forget it."

He sat down next to Garth on the sofa. "Listen, pal," he said. "Your mother and I have been talking, and I've managed to convince her to take a little time off. So we're going camping."

"Really?"

"Really. To Maine. All of us."

"But without Joan, right?"

"Of course without Joan," said his father, looking at him oddly.

"Great!"

# CHAPTER FOUR

# Are We Having Fun Yet?

That week Garth and Mr. Hunter spent a lot of time getting ready for their trip. They fixed the zipper on the tent. They bought trail mix. They put new batteries in the flashlights. And they bought Garth a new sleeping bag, because his old one was too small for him. It had been at least three years since they'd gone camping.

"Remember how much fun we used to have?" asked Mr. Hunter as he and Garth drove to the supermarket Thursday to buy marshmallows. "Remember how you always used to get melted marshmallows all over your clothes?"

"Mmm," said Garth. "That was B.P." This was code for "Before Ph.D."—a term only he and his father used.

"Things will be fun again," said Mr. Hunter. "A.P."

"After Ph.D.?"

"You got it."

That seemed like a long, long time away.

Garth's mother got home after eight that night. "I'm too tired to eat," she said, letting her heavy canvas bag full of books and papers drop to the floor. "I'll just have some cereal and go up to bed, okay?"

"Gee," said Garth's father, who was cooking cheese sauce at the stove. "Garth and I were turning out a nice dinner here." Garth was sitting at the kitchen table, cutting tomatoes for a salad.

His mother sighed. Heavily. "Okay," she said, sounding as if she were being forced to walk the plank. "Okay. It's just that I have so much work to finish up before the weekend because we're going away."

Mr. Hunter kept stirring the sauce. "Oh. So spending time with your family is causing terrible problems for you," he said.

"I didn't say that."

"We don't have to go camping," he said. He threw the spoon into the sink. "Come to think of it, we don't have to do *anything* together." He walked out of the room. A minute later the back door slammed.

Garth stared at his bowl of tomatoes, stunned. His dad almost never lost his temper. It was awful, the way his parents were fighting. It scared him.

His mother walked over and kissed him on the forehead. "Keep cutting tomatoes," she said. "I'll go talk to him."

Ten minutes later they were back in the kitchen. They both looked tired.

"Storm's over, pal," Garth's father told him. But Garth still felt uneasy. Even though everybody tried to act cheerful at the table, he could tell it was an effort. What kind of camping trip was this going to be, anyway?

Weekend of Doom, thought Garth unhappily.

To make matters worse, Joan wove back and forth under the table, meowing at him. She knew he couldn't answer back, no matter what.

"So," she said. "Looks like a great trip coming up, doesn't it? Everybody's in such a *great* mood. Wish I was coming along, don't you?"

Garth dropped his napkin and then leaned down to pick it up. "Brat!" he snapped at her.

"Me?" she protested. "Why, I'm as good as gold. A saint. I haven't touched your friend Weebie. Yet."

Garth could feel Weebie trembling in his pocket. "Don't you dare!" he whispered to her.

"What?" said Mr. Hunter.

Garth straightened up. "Oh, nothing," he said. "Just clearing my throat." He shot Joan a warning look. In reply she stationed herself just out of his reach. But he could still hear her purring.

\* \* \*

After the dishes were washed, Garth's mother went into the den to study, and Garth went up to his room. He was reading a comic with Weebie perched on his chest when there was a knock on the door. He put Weebie in his cage and settled on his bed again.

"Come on in, Dad," he called.

Mr. Hunter came in holding a letter and something that looked like a diagram. "Here's a map of the campground," he said. "I got it in the mail today. Thought you could help me pick out a good site."

"Sure," said Garth. He knew his dad was trying to make him feel better about the trip. They looked at the map together for a moment.

"How about this one?" said Mr. Hunter.

"I don't know," said Garth. "Look how close it is to the outhouse. There'll be people going by all the time."

"You're right," said his father. "Good thinking."

"How about this one?" said Garth, pointing to a site all the way at the edge of the

campground. "It's right near the lake. That might be cool."

His father examined the map. "Looks good," he said. "Though it's a little far from the nearest outhouse. That okay for you?"

"Sure."

"All right! I'll reserve it tomorrow. Then Saturday, we're off!"

# A Really Great Beginning

Saturday morning dawned chilly and gray. Garth and his parents started packing their gear into the station wagon at six, and by six thirty they were ready to go. Garth settled into the backseat as his parents loaded the last few things onto the roof rack. He checked his waist pack, where Weebie was tucked away.

"You okay, Weeb?" he asked softly.

"Okay as I'll ever be," said Weebie. "Can't say I really like the idea of going into the woods, though. Too many snakes."

"Can't you talk to them? Ask them to leave you alone?"

"Get real!" snorted Weebie. "They're not interested in chatting. They're interested in swallowing you whole."

"Oh." Garth didn't have time to worry about which place was more dangerous for Weebie—in the woods with snakes, or at home with Joan. At that moment his parents climbed into the car, and they were off.

They got all the way to Massachusetts in silence. Garth's mother stared out the window, frowning. Garth's father stared straight ahead, driving.

Finally Garth's father spoke. "Want to play a game?" he asked.

Nobody answered.

"How about Ghost?" he persisted.

"Okay," said Garth halfheartedly.

"You two play," said his mother. "I need to memorize the twelve symptoms of acute depression."

Mr. Hunter looked into the rearview mirror. "You start, pal," he said.

"P," said Garth.

"L," said his father.

"A."

"T."

Uh-oh. All Garth could think of was "E," which would end the word "plate" on him. That meant he'd lose the first round. He thought some more.

Aha! If he said "T" to make the word "platter," that would end up on . . . let's see . . . Garth. Rats.

He thought some more. There didn't seem to be any way out of it.

"Y!" squeaked Weebie from the waist pack.

"Huh?" said Garth.

"I didn't say anything," said Mr. Hunter.

"Y!" repeated Weebie. "You can make the word 'platypus'! It ends on your father!"

Garth worked it out in his head. Weebie was right. "Where'd you learn to spell?" he whispered.

"I spent my whole life in a third-grade classroom, dim bulb," said Weebie.

"What?" said Mr. Hunter.

"Y!" called Garth triumphantly.

Mr. Hunter raised his eyebrows. Then he

thought for five minutes. Finally he smiled into the mirror at Garth. "Brilliant, pal," he said. "I give up. You get a G."

"All right!" crowed Garth.

"We must learn to be gracious in victory," his father reminded him.

They played for a long time after that, and with Weebie's help, Garth got out of lots of tight spots. He finally lost, but by much less than usual. Then he and his father played spot-the-license-plate until they got to Maine. Pretty soon they'd reached the Happy Valley Campground.

Mr. Hunter pulled the car up to the office and went in to register. Garth and Mrs. Hunter got out of the car to stretch their legs.

It started to drizzle.

"Oh, great," said Mrs. Hunter. The drizzle turned to rain, and she pulled up the hood of her sweatshirt. For a minute she looked just like an unhappy turtle. Then she sneezed. "Oh, no!" she moaned. "I'm getting a cold!"

Garth pulled his cap down and his shirt collar up. He didn't know what to say, so he climbed back into the car after his mother. A minute later his father came out of the office carrying some papers. "We're set," he said. "Site number sixty-three, all the way at the end."

They drove down a winding dirt road in the rain, windshield wipers squeaking all the way. The campground seemed deserted. Or else people were in their tents, trying to stay dry.

Just beyond a bend in the road Garth saw the marker. "Look!" he said. "There it is— number sixty-three." Mr. Hunter stopped the car and they all climbed out.

They could tell right away it was a really nice campsite—large, flat, and carpeted with pine needles. Off to one side was a circle of stones for a campfire. Just beyond it the surface of the lake gleamed in the rain.

"Okay," said Mr. Hunter in his heartiest voice. "Let's get this tent up. What do you say, pal?"

"Fine, Dad." Garth pulled out their rain ponchos, and they put them on.

"Why don't you stay in the car?" Mr. Hunter said to his wife. "No sense in all of us getting wet."

"Thanks," she said gratefully. "I think I will."

Garth and his dad set to work. They were a little out of practice, so for a while Mr. Hunter stood in the rain holding a bunch of metal pole sections and thinking. The sections were supposed to fit together and hold up the tent. Once Mr. Hunter remembered how to put them together, Garth's job was to pound the pegs into the ground with a rock.

Weebie was quiet in the waist pack.

More rain fell.

"Let's see," said Mr. Hunter, after several minutes of deep thought. "This one should go into that one, and that one should go through the loop on the tent, and . . . *OW!*"

"What happened?" asked Garth.

"Pinched my finger. No big deal," said Mr. Hunter, dancing up and down in slow motion and sucking on his hand.

An hour later the tent was finally assembled. Garth's mother was still reading in the car.

"Nola," Mr. Hunter called. "Tent's ready."

Mrs. Hunter looked up from her book,

startled. When she saw the tent, she opened the car door and ran for it, clutching her book tightly with both arms. Once she was inside, she sneezed four times.

Garth and Mr. Hunter heard her blow her nose.

"Thanks for setting this up, guys," she called out to them.

"No problem," said Mr. Hunter in a too-cheerful voice. "We'll just finish up now." He smiled wanly at Garth. Garth just managed to smile back.

For the next hour they unloaded the car. They carried the sleeping bags, their duffel, and their lantern into the tent, and then unpacked the food. Mr. Hunter put most of it into a cooler that he wrapped with a bungee cord. He took the rest and hung it up in a little hammock between two trees.

"What's that for?" asked Garth.

"To keep it away from raccoons," said his father. "And bears. They steal food."

"Bears? There are bears around here?"

"Could be. You never know."

Garth felt a thrill of excitement mixed with a little fear. "Bears," he said. "Cool."

"We probably won't see any," said his father reassuringly. "But speaking of food, we should start thinking about dinner. You hungry?"

Garth nodded. He was.

"Me too," said Mr. Hunter. "If you can scare up some dry wood, I'll get a fire going."

"Deal," said Garth, heading for the trees. But finding kindling turned out to be really hard. In fact, it turned out to be impossible. In the woods the ground was completely wet, and water dripped steadily from every leaf and branch, even though it had stopped coming down from the sky.

As hard as he looked, Garth could find only four pieces of wood that weren't soaking wet. His father was pretty good at making fires. Maybe he could use these.

He couldn't. After twenty minutes of hunching over the sticks, lighting them, blowing on them, even pleading with them, he gave up.

"I noticed a little general store just outside

the campground," he said to Garth. "Maybe we can get some sandwiches there."

They left Garth's mother reading in the tent and started hiking. Before too long they were back with cheese sandwiches, root beer, potato chips, and licorice sticks. Garth had even managed to buy some honey-roasted peanuts for Weebie.

"Yummy dinner!" called Garth's father. "Come and get it."

"Be right out," called Mrs. Hunter. "I'm just finishing a chapter."

Garth stuck his head into the tent. His mother was stretched out on an air mattress with a huge book propped up on her stomach. "What are you reading, anyway?" he asked.

She held the book so he could see the title: *Paranoia from A to Z.*

"Looks exciting," said Garth.

"Well, it is," she said. "Just give me another minute, okay?"

Fifteen minutes later, Garth and his father decided they were too hungry to wait. They ate their sandwiches and the potato chips, and they were just starting on the licorice when Mrs. Hunter emerged from the tent.

"Here I am," she said.

"We're done," said Garth's father.

"Sorry, guys," she said. Then she looked down at the picnic table. "Cheese sandwiches?" she said. "This is the yummy dinner?"

Garth's father jumped up. "That's it!" he cried. "I've had it! I'm going for a walk. Want to come, Garth?"

Garth didn't know what to say. If he went with his father, it would seem like he was taking sides against his mother. He didn't want that. But he didn't really want to stay with her, either.

There was the gentlest of stirrings from inside his waist pack, and Garth knew then who he wanted to talk to. "No thanks, Dad," he said. "I'm just gonna sit by the lake for a while."

He grabbed one last licorice stick and left.

53

·······························

# Somebody
# New

Once he was safely out of sight, Garth took Weebie out of his pack and set him on the ground.

"Don't go anywhere," he said.

"If I went anywhere, I'd get eaten by a snake. I'm sticking with you," said Weebie.

Garth stared at the water. "What if they get a divorce?" he said. His voice cracked a little.

"They won't get a divorce. They're just going through a rough patch," said Weebie.

"I hope you're right," said Garth. "I don't

want to have underwear in two houses like my friend Jeremy."

"You won't, you won't. Your parents just have to remember how to be nice to each other, that's all. They have to remember that they like each other."

"Yeah, well they definitely forgot that." Garth and Weebie watched the lake for a long time in silence. The sun set. The lake went from orange to purple to gray as night fell. Garth sighed. He didn't want to go back to the campsite, but his parents would worry now that it was dark.

He stood up. "I have to go to the bathroom," he told Weebie. "I think the outhouse is . . . hmmm . . ." He looked around, trying to remember the map. "Uh, there." He pointed to his left, toward the woods. "Can't be too far." He put Weebie in his pocket and set off.

Soon it was *really* dark, and Garth began to have trouble following the path. Wet greenery smacked him in the face and chest as he walked. Like punishment, he thought gloomily.

"Are you sure this is the right way?" asked Weebie.

"I think so," Garth said, but he wasn't sure at all.

There was the loud crack of a branch snapping nearby. They froze. "What was that?" whispered Weebie.

"I don't know," Garth whispered back. They stood there listening. The wind made its way through the trees. Leaves rustled. One bullfrog honked to another. "Probably nothing," Garth decided. "A deer, maybe."

They kept walking. The moon rose, shrouded in haze. Garth wished he had a flashlight.

Then he saw . . . something. "What's that big thing over there?" he asked Weebie.

"Where?"

"There! On the right! That big thing. See?"

Weebie poked his head up. "That? That's a—might be a big tree stump. Or maybe a—"

"BEAR . . . !?" moaned Garth as it turned to face them. "Oh, no!"

It was a bear all right, a big black one. It looked about a hundred feet tall, like a shaggy hill on legs, and it was eating berries.

"Quick!" demanded Garth. "What are you supposed to do when you meet a bear? Stand still or run?"

"Uh . . . um . . . I don't think Ms. Wackerow ever covered that," said Weebie.

"RROOOWWW!" roared the bear.

"Omigosh!" croaked Garth. "I'm too young to die."

"OOOWWW!" The bear was coming closer. Garth broke out in a sweat.

"Just a second," Weebie said. He stood up as tall as he could and called out to the bear. "DID YOU SAY 'OW'?" he asked.

"Yeah. I did," answered the bear in a deep, raspy voice.

Garth's skin prickled. "Holy cow!" he said. "I can understand him! I can understand bears!"

Weebie ignored Garth. "And why did you say 'ow'?" he called out to the bear. "Can you tell me?"

"My paw hurts," said the bear in his deep voice. "Look. I'll show you." He lumbered over to them with surprising speed. Garth backed away a little. The bear's smell—like wet earth, dirty socks, and honey—made his eyes water.

"Lookit." The bear stuck out his paw.

Nervous but fascinated, Garth leaned closer, struggling to see in the dim light. A long fat thorn, about as thick as a toothpick, was stuck in the tender pad of the bear's paw.

"Whoa, that's a bad one," said Garth.

"It's almost as big as me," said Weebie.

"It hurts something terrible," said the bear.

"You know what?" said Garth. "I think I can help you." He unzipped his waist pack and poked around in it. "My father gave me a first-aid kit, and I'm pretty sure there's a pair of tweezers in it. Ah! There it is."

He pulled out the little plastic box, which held aspirin, gauze, tape, and, yes—a pair of tweezers. He looked into the bear's dark eyes. "Can you hold your paw still?" he asked. He wouldn't let himself think about the bear's long, curving claws, which looked as sharp and black as iron nails.

"I'll try real, real hard," said the bear earnestly. "Will it hurt?"

"No," said Garth. Then he thought of all the times he'd asked that very same question, and of how grown-ups always said no. He reached out and patted the bear's paw.

"It might hurt just a little, but only for a second, okay? Ready?"

The bear closed his eyes. "Ready."

Garth took hold of the thorn firmly with the tweezers and yanked.

"YOW!" roared the bear, dancing backward.

"All done," said Garth.

"Honest?"

"Honest. Look." Garth showed him the thorn, which really was as long as Weebie. The bear flexed his paw, then batted it back and forth a few times. "It's gone!" he roared. "It doesn't hurt no more!"

"Anymore," corrected Weebie.

"Sorry. Anymore. Anyhow, you fixed it. This is great! How can I thank you?"

"Hey, it was nothing," said Garth. "Don't worry about—"

"Hold on," interrupted Weebie. "Would you really like to do something for us?" he asked.

"Yeah! Sure!" said the bear eagerly.

Weebie turned to Garth. "Remember how we were talking about your parents before? About their rough patch? And how they had to be reminded that they liked each other?"

"Yes . . . ?"

"Well, I just had an idea," said Weebie. "Listen to this, guys. . . ."

# Weebie's Plan

The bear told Garth where the outhouse was, and five minutes later Garth was back at the campsite. His parents were sitting at the picnic table looking worried. They jumped up when they saw him.

"Garth!" cried his mother. "Where have you been?"

"Just looking for the outhouse. It was really dark."

"Don't you ever, *ever* wander off like that again!" she said. Now that she wasn't scared anymore, she was angry. "We've been worried sick about you!"

"Sorry," said Garth. "I won't do it again."

"You better not," said his father. "If you know what's good for you, pal."

"I promise, I promise," said Garth. He sat down at the table and helped himself to the last licorice stick. "So," he said innocently, "what's new?"

His mother managed a smile. "I finished studying," she said. "Finally." She patted her book, which sat on the bench beside her.

"Hey, that's great, Mom," said Garth.

"And the weather's improved," said his father. It looked as if, in Garth's absence, they had decided to make the best of things. Now they were working hard to be cheerful.

"Let's tell stories," suggested Mrs. Hunter.

"Perfect!" said Mr. Hunter. "Who's got a good one?"

"You do, Toby," said his wife. "Remember that story you told me about the house in the woods? The haunted one? In northern Westchester?"

"Oh . . . yeah," said Mr. Hunter. "That is

pretty good. Okay, here goes." He turned down the lantern a little.

"Deep, deep in the Katonah woods, surrounded by gnarly old trees," he began, "is a deserted house. Its paint is peeling. Its doors and windows are thick with cobwebs. And at night strange, echoey, moaning sounds come from deep inside it, almost as if it were in pain—"

*CRASH!*

"What on earth was that?" cried Garth's mother.

"I don't know," said Garth's father. "But it sounded very close."

"And very big," said Garth's mother.

They heard another crash, even closer this time. And then there he was, right next to them—a huge black bear. He looked about a hundred feet tall, and his dark eyes glittered.

*"GROOOAARRR!"* said the bear.

Garth's mother screamed.

The bear waved his paws in the air and showed his teeth. *"GROOOAARRR!"* he said again. Then he whacked at the food hanging from the trees. The little hammock ripped.

Garth's father stood up. Garth and his mother sat there, frozen. The bear looked terrifying.

"*AARRRR!*" he roared, swatting at the hammock again, bringing down three oranges and a bunch of bananas—the family breakfast.

"Hey!" shouted Mr. Hunter. "Stop that!" The bear, who was reaching out for the bananas, stopped. Then he growled and rushed at Mr. Hunter, baring his teeth.

Garth's stomach tightened. The bear looked so angry! And he was waving his claws within an inch of Mr. Hunter's nose!

"NO!" Suddenly Garth's mother jumped to her feet and was shouting at the bear. "Get away! Don't you hurt him!"

"It's working!" squeaked Weebie. "See?"

"Is it?" whispered Garth. He was so scared, he could hardly get the words out. "I don't think the bear's really fooling, do you?"

"Don't worry," said Weebie. "He's being very careful."

"Nola!" called Garth's father as the bear loomed over him. "Don't come any closer! Stay back!" Garth had never seen his father so pale.

Mrs. Hunter's eyes went from her husband to the bear and back to her husband. Then, suddenly, she moved. She grabbed *Paranoia from A to Z* with both hands and heaved it straight at the bear. "Don't touch my husband!" she shouted.

The heavy book bounced off the bear's nose. Garth and Weebie both winced.

The bear stopped roaring immediately. He backed away, looking slightly puzzled. Then he rubbed his nose with his paw, turned, and shambled off into the woods.

Garth's parents stood there, panting.

Then they reached for each other and hugged, hard.

"I don't ever want to lose you, Toby," said Mrs. Hunter.

He patted her on the back. "You won't," he promised.

Weebie poked Garth with his nose. "Everything's going to be all right," he said.

The next morning Garth told his parents, who were holding hands at breakfast, that he was going to the outhouse. In fact he and Weebie wanted to find the bear.

The woods were a lot less scary in the day-light. Their endless, confused wandering of the night before was now just a short walk down a shady path.

"Where's that berry patch?" wondered Garth.

"Over there!" squeaked Weebie, pointing his tiny paw. "See it?"

A dense clump of bushes bordered the path on their right. And there, gulping down whole branches—berries, leaves, and all—was their friend.

"Hi," said Garth.

"Oh, hiya," said the bear.

"I came to thank you," said Garth. "You did a great job last night—totally convincing."

"It was nothing," said the bear modestly.

"How's your nose?" Garth inquired. "I'm really sorry about that. Mom got carried away."

"Just a little bump," said the bear. "It'll be fine."

"Well, thanks again," said Garth.

"Glad to help," said the bear.

Garth turned to leave. "By the way," he said, "what's your name?"

The bear looked at him. "I'm a bear," he said. "I live in the woods. Nobody here needs a name."

And with that he went back to eating.

# CHAPTER EIGHT

# Weebie Stays

The rest of the summer was a big improvement. Garth's mother still worked a lot, but things were different at home. She was around more, she paid more attention to Garth, and she and Mr. Hunter were getting along a lot better. They still argued, but the arguments weren't as serious as before. After a while Garth stopped worrying about them. They were definitely not getting divorced—he could tell.

"Nothing like a near-death experience to bring folks together," said Weebie. He was a lot more relaxed these days, too, thanks to the agreement between Garth and Joan.

Garth had figured out how to keep Joan away from Weebie. "Look," he had said to her when the family got back from camping, "I have a proposition for you."

Joan waved her tail at him. "Better be good," she said, eyeing Weebie's cage. "I'm hungry."

"It is good," said Garth. "If you promise to keep away from Weebie, I'll feed you every day—I swear. And I'll feed you anything you like! Except live rodents," he added hastily.

Joan sat down and licked her paw for a long time. Garth knew she was thinking it over.

"Coffee ice cream?" she asked.

"Yes."

"Raw chicken livers?"

Garth tried not to gag. "Yes."

"Shrimp with black bean sauce?"

"Anything!" said Garth. "Just leave him alone, okay?"

"Two-month trial period," said Joan. "Slip up once, he's my supper."

"One month."

"Six weeks, end of discussion."

It was a deal.

The summer flew by, and September got closer and closer. Garth knew he had to start thinking about taking Weebie back to school. He hated the idea. So, it turned out, did Weebie.

"Do I have to go back?" he squeaked. "I like it so much better here. Nobody squeezes me too hard. I get nature shows on TV, and chocolate chips, and rock and roll. And I get you! Please don't take me back there."

Garth knew he had to do something. So one day near the end of August, he found Ms. Wackerow's number in the phone book and called her.

"Oh, hi, Garth," she said. "It's nice to hear from you. How are you doing with Weebie?"

Garth said they were doing so well that he wanted to keep Weebie.

"Really!" Ms. Wackerow sounded surprised but pleased. "You want the responsibility? That's so good! What about your parents? Is it all right with them?"

"I'm sure it's fine with them," said Garth. He told Ms. Wackerow about feeding Joan as well as Weebie, and how happy his parents were about it. This was true. They had even raised his allowance.

"Well, wonderful," said Ms. Wackerow.

"But what about the rest of the children? They'll miss Weebie."

Garth had thought about this and talked it over with Weebie. "I'll bring him in for show and tell," he said. "A lot."

"Hmmm," said Ms. Wackerow. "All right," she said at last. "He's yours."

"Thanks, Ms. Wackerow!" said Garth. He ran back to his room and scooped Weebie out of his cage.

"It's you and me!" he said. "You don't have to go back!"

"Great!" squeaked Weebie, flinging his little arms wide.

To celebrate, Garth took Weebie to the pet store and bought him the mermaid he'd admired.

"I think I'll call her Wanda," said Weebie. "Or maybe Nortrude. What do you think?"

"I think if people knew I was walking down the street talking to a gerbil, they'd lock me up somewhere."

"It is pretty great, isn't it?" said Weebie. "A boy who can talk to animals."

"Well, gerbils, cats, and bears, anyhow."

"Just wait till you get to know a few toads," said Weebie. "Big complainers—but very, very funny."

And they made their way home, talking about all kinds of things.

## DATE DUE